EMILY L.

Other works by Marguerite Duras
published by Pantheon:

THE LOVER
THE RAVISHING OF LOL STEIN
THE SAILOR FROM GIBRALTAR
THE WAR
THE VICE-CONSUL
L'AMANTE ANGLAISE
BLUE EYES, BLACK HAIR

MARGUERITE DURAS

EMILY L.

Translated from the French by Barbara Bray

PANTHEON BOOKS, NEW YORK

First American Edition

Translation Copyright © 1989 by Random House, Inc.

All rights reserved under International and Pan-American Copyright
Conventions. Published in the United States by Pantheon Books, a
division of Random House, Inc., New York, and simultaneously in
Canada by Random House of Canada Limited, Toronto. Originally
published in France by Les Editions de Minuit. Copyright © 1987
by Les Editions de Minuit.

Library of Congress Cataloging-in-Publication Data

Duras, Marguerite.
  Emily L.

  I. Title.
PQ2607.U8245E4513 1989 843'.912 88-43107
ISBN 0-394-57233-5

Book Design by Gina Davis
MANUFACTURED IN THE UNITED STATES OF AMERICA

FOR JEAN MASCOLO

EMILY L.

IT BEGAN WITH THE FEAR.

We'd driven to Quillebeuf, as we often did that summer.

We got there at the usual time, late afternoon. As usual we went for a stroll beside the white rail that runs along the quayside from the church at the entrance to the harbor to the disused path that leads out of it, probably to the forest of Brotonne.

We look at the tanker port on the other side of the river, and at the tall cliffs of Le Havre in the distance, and at the sky. Then at the red ferry crossing and the people being taken across the river. And all the time,

3

frail and white, fencing off the water, there's the rail.

We go and sit on the terrace outside the Hôtel de la Marine, in the middle of the square, opposite the ramp leading onto the ferry.

The tables are in the shadow of the hotel buildings. The air is still. There's no wind.

I look at you. You're looking at the place. The heat. The flat waters of the river. The summer. And then you look past all that. With your hands, your beautiful white hands, clasped under your chin, you look without seeing. Without moving, you ask me what's the matter. I answer as usual. Nothing's the matter. I'm just looking at you.

You don't move at first, then from where I'm sitting I can see a smile in your eyes. You say, "You like this place. One day it'll all be in a book—the square, the heat, the river."

I don't answer. I don't know. I tell you I don't know in advance, or only very rarely.

The square is empty. The ferry is full of tourists. The Seine valley ends here, this is the last ferry after Jumièges. As soon as the ferry leaves, the square is empty again. It's between two landings of the ferry, while the square is empty, that fear arrives. I look

4

around and suddenly there are people on the other side of the square, at the entrance to the disused path, where there shouldn't be anybody at all. They've stopped and are looking at us. About fifteen of them, all dressed alike, in white. The same person multiplied indefinitely. I look away.

I look again and see I was mistaken. They're still there, but they've come closer. Some of them are talking. Inaudibly as yet, but I know now they do exist. I can see the details. To me they're clearly murderers, but I recognize this fear, whereas I don't know anything about the one before. They seem to have only one face: all their faces are the same, that's why they're so frightening. They've all got crew-cuts, slanting eyes, the same cheerful expression; they're all of the same build, the same height. But that's not what's wrong—that's unusual but not unheard-of. I say, "Why are there Koreans in Quillebeuf?"

You turn towards me quickly. You must have sensed the fear just from the sudden change in my voice.

"Where can you see any Koreans?"

"You've got your back to them. Look behind you, at the end of the quay."

You turned around, paused long enough to realize

5

what it meant to me. You too were afraid the things of the night might start appearing to me again. You tried to think what to say: I understood you too.

You said, "Yes, they're Asiatics. But why Koreans, necessarily?"

"I don't know. I've never seen one."

You suddenly laugh. I join in. You say, "And as you've never seen one, you think any Asiatics you don't recognize must be Koreans—is that it?"

"Yes."

You looked at some length in the direction of the Koreans. Then you turned and looked at me so deeply and intently you didn't see me at all. All of a sudden the idea that I existed entered your mind. You looked at me as if you loved me. You used to do that sometimes.

I say there's nothing I can do about this fear. I can't escape it. I can't find out what it is.

You aren't listening to what I say. You keep looking at me with an expression I've never seen in anyone but you.

The Koreans have come nearer and sat down at some of the other tables. They look at us as we were looking at them a moment ago. They smile a cruel smile that suddenly gives way to what seems an insurmountable sadness. Then the cruel smile returns to each face. And stays there, fixed in the eyes and half-open mouth. It was the smile that was frightening, that foretold the massacres I anticipated. I, the woman in this story, the woman in Quillebeuf this afternoon with you, the man looking at me.

I was still afraid, even though I said no more about it. You knew. That amused you too. You said, "Lousy racist." I said you were right. I'd said what I think. I couldn't help laughing, either.

I said, "Death will be Japanese. The death of the world. It will come from Korea. That's what I think. *You* may have time to see it in action."

You said it was possible.

As the Koreans showed no sign of leaving the terrace, you said we'd better go inside the café. You'd seen that I was watching them, that the fear was still there. And you knew it was no use arguing, and that, as I'd admit later on in a book, I was as hopeless an idiot as ever. I followed you into the café. I always followed you everywhere, wherever you went.

The Café de la Marine was almost empty that afternoon, apart from the regular customers—local peo-

7

ple and young men who'd come over on the ferry. We knew most of them by sight. They were in the main room of the Marine with the manageress and a young woman who was probably her daughter. A lot of the young men worked in the tanker port on the other side of the river, and must have been in the habit of calling in at the Marine on the way home to their villages in the marshes. There were some tourists too, from Ceylon you said, and others of various nationalities. Some of them could understand a bit of French and laughed politely but tentatively at the young men's jokes. Others obviously couldn't understand a word, and gazed at the hotel menu, the square, and the people with the same bemused smile. It was a pity such coarse and rowdy conversation should be inflicted on these forlorn transients. But apart from that, the Hôtel de la Marine bar was nice and peaceful.

We'd taken them in, the couple at the bar, in the same way as we'd taken in the customers in the main room and the manageress and the young woman with her. And it went on like that for quite a while. They'd been there when we came into the café, there was no reason why we should notice them, and then suddenly we must have seen them. We must have looked

8

at them first without seeing them, and then all of a sudden have seen them. And not have been able to do anything else ever since.

First separately. And then both of them at once. Merged together into one color, one form. One age.

Of their own accord they'd gone to the end of the bar reserved for strangers. The regular customers were at the other end, nearest the main room. They, those two, were alone. Lost. Alone in the summer, in the wilderness. Lost amid the light reflected from the river onto the square, the walls, the chalk cliffs, and the double doors of the bar, wide open to the air outside. They didn't see anyone or anything. Neither the summer light nor the river.

In front of them were the sort of drinks hard drinkers from England and America go in for: a dark Pilsen for him, a double bourbon for her.

Perched on their barstools almost motionless, their heads hanging forward, they looked slightly ridiculous. Like plants, or some objects not quite one thing or the other. Human plants or vegetables, no sooner born than blighted, no sooner living than dead. Yes, things innocent yet punished. Trees. Trees deprived of soil and water. But doomed to slump in the form of humans, there before our eyes.

At first I thought she, the woman at the bar, was

asleep. But I don't think so now. I think she just had her eyes shut. But she kept her head raised so as to hear the voices around her better, especially those in the main room, some of which were from England. She listened to the sound of those voices, and to what they were saying in their own kind of English.

They too, the couple, were genuine English people from England. When silence fell in the main room, you could sometimes hear the kind of English they spoke to one another. You couldn't make out all of it. They didn't carry on a continuous conversation. They just spoke from time to time, and so quietly that the slightest thing, just a snatch of a distant voice, was enough to drown it. But from the little you could hear, it seemed they were upset at not being able to get away; the engine of some vehicle or other had broken down. Unless the problem was some journey they'd planned, which this hitch had forced them to abandon. They occasionally mentioned various technical terms, but they didn't seem too happy with them. And they soon gave up the struggle.

But at one point they did mention a boat.

And another time they referred to the sea.

In the time it takes to say it, a gust of wind swept

across the harbor and then dropped. "*The turn of the tide,*" he said. "*The sea must be marvelously calm. As it sometimes is in summer.*"*

She listened. And smiled, pleased that the sea was calm.

Where did it come from, the fascination, the grace, whatever the word is, of the time, the place, those people? It's impossible to say. I don't know. Probably from their humility in the face of death. But also from their lack of shame. And from what had happened. From all these things at once, and from each one separately. But there's no saying why or how. From the river too, and the light over everything, and the whiteness shed everywhere by the white cliffs. From the white of the chalk, of the cliffs, of the spray. Of the gulls—a white mixed with blue. And of the wind.

There's no way of knowing their age. But you can see she's appreciably older than he. And that he has caught up with her slowness and won't outstrip it, and that it's been like this for years. It's all over for her, and yet she's still there with him, her body still

---

*Dialogue printed in italics is in English in the original.—TRANS.

within reach of his, of his hands, everywhere, night and day.

It was clear it was all over, and at the same time that she was still there. And this was clear too: that if he ever left her she'd just stay there and die where it happened.

That's how it began for us with those people at the bar: with their deliberate immobility. He looking at her, or sometimes into the mirror behind the bar when the red ferry came in and its passengers went past the hotel. And she looking only at the floor.

On the bar in front of them stood the empty bottle of strong black Pilsen and the glass of whiskey, the ice melting now. They must have drunk quite a lot before we came into the Café de la Marine.

I spoke to you. I said I'd decided to write our story. You didn't react. You went on looking at the woman as if you hadn't realized it was you I was talking to.

I said it again—that I was going to write the story of the affair we'd had together, the one that was still there and taking forever to die.

You looked out at the river, but not seeing it, or anything, for a long time. Apprehensive.

"That again . . . I don't believe it."

"I haven't decided anything . . . But that's not the point. I can't stop writing. I can't. And when I'm writing the story it's as if I were back with you again, back at a time when I don't know yet what's happening or what's going to happen . . . who you are or what is going to become of us."

In your eyes there's a flash of guile, fear, and deep down, a passion for living. You say, "I bet you're writing it at this very moment. Don't deny it."

"No, I don't think so. But I've been thinking about it for such a long time. Two years at least—I forget. To tell you the truth, I forget. But I don't think it's our story I'm writing. Four years after, it can't be the same. It's not the same now, and later on it will be even more different. No. What I'm writing now is something else that will somehow include it—something much broader, perhaps. But to write about it directly—no, that's all over, I couldn't do it now."

You don't look at me. You've been trying to provoke me. But now your fierce expression is engulfed in a kind of woe. You say, "There's nothing to tell. Nothing. Nothing ever happened."

I answer after a pause, "Sometimes talking to each other is as difficult as dying."

"Yes."

"When it's in a book I don't think it'll hurt any

more . . . exist any more. It'll be wiped out. That's what I find, with this story I've had with you. That writing . . . one of the things writing does is wipe things out. Replace them."

"Death doesn't wipe anything out—I'll say that. When you die, the story will become legendary, flagrant."

I look at you again. You've gone slightly pale—there, around the lips. Very slightly. But unmistakably.

I give up on you. At the same moment I stop talking to you forever and speak to you for the first time.

"There must be a way of saying what you say, of arriving at the certainty it gives you such pleasure to believe in—that nothing ever happened. Once that was established one could wait for all the rest, accept what the two lovers might not have perceived at the time. For example, that you didn't feel any desire for me, but at the same time . . . at the same time . . ."

"That's when it ought to be clear whether or not there's anything to be done with what has"—you smile—"or hasn't happened."

I look at you. I say, "Strange that you don't understand. It makes no difference whether what's left

14

then, at that moment, comes from what has happened or from what one thinks has happened. But now there's nothing to divide us"—it's my turn to smile—"we've both reached the same point."

"You mean . . . You're talking about what's left now—at this stage . . . this summer—of what someone chose to imagine once, years ago."

I look at you. I say you don't know. I tell you, "Something did happen the first day."

You hesitate. And then you say, "No, nothing. Nothing happened, ever."

"You just didn't know."

We don't say anything.

We look at the river.

The ferry is almost empty. The heat feels suddenly heavy, oppressive. The absence of wind is becoming unbearable.

You say, "You imagined for me. I had no hand in the story you had with me."

"You said the opposite once. At the beginning."

"I say anything, and then I forget. You know that." You smile. "But I'm always there when you're in the despair I've driven you to."

"I know. And I know that for me, even if you said it without thinking, just to please me, it's the same as if you'd said it for always. It's there. And it's because someone said that other thing that other day that the book will be written. The book will tell the truth. Whether we said it ourselves or heard it said through a wall, by someone other than you to some-one other than me, it will be all the same as far as the book is concerned, so long as you heard it at the same time I did and in the same place. In the same fear."

We fall silent. You start looking at the river again, and then at the room and the woman at the bar looking down at the floor. You say, "You mustn't believe what I say. Don't write any more."

"I do believe all you say, even the things that are most untrue, even your lies. I believe in the whole of what you say, every word, even if it's absent-minded or idiotic. I even believe in your overriding sincerity amid all that farrago."

"Don't write any more."

"When I write, I don't love you any more."

We look at one another. Then away. I say, "Words like that are frightening."

"Yes."

"Incredible how close one can get to despair. When one is talking, I mean."

"Yes."

You smile. You've turned pale again, just there around the lips, only slightly, but once more it's unmistakable.

I say, "I don't love you any more. It's you who love me. But you don't know it."

We go over to the rail. We look at the river.

"It's complicated."

"Yes."

We come back into the bar. The manageress is serving a black Pilsen and a double bourbon to the English travelers. We stand in the doorway, a long way away from them. Suddenly, a long way away from everything.

All that summer, three or four times a week, we used to go to Quillebeuf. We went out every day. Love was too near or too far, we couldn't tell which—the day was bound to come when we couldn't tell which. That was another reason why we kept going to Quillebeuf: so as not to be shut up indoors together with despair.

At first we had several different ways, four or five of them, of getting to Quillebeuf. Then in the end we kept to just one, the one through Pont-Audemer. We drove through the town and its various squares and then, instead of going straight up the road that crosses the plateau, we turned left, towards the west, onto a little road that went around the plateau, along by the river Risle. As soon as we left Pont-Audemer the summer began for us, with water everywhere— the river, the canals, the sodden fields, the eel fishers, the boathouses, and far away in front of us, moon-colored, the estuary of the Risle. After the water we reached the hill, by way of a dark lane almost frightening because of the denseness of the trees. Sometimes we switched the headlights on.

You start to be in Quillebeuf as soon as you're up on the chalk plateau. Every turn in the road brings you out of dark forest into a patch of brilliant sun— one of the clearings made in the dampness of the forest for grazing in years of bad weather. Then you leave the light and go back again into the dark, and shout with joy because that too is where summer begins. In the alternations of darkness and light. In the flowing streams. In the brook-fed marshes, fertile as gardens. It's here among the fields and the grey elms that the daily flood occurs, towards the swirling estuary.

The young river was here first, but the sea accepted salt and fresh water alike, rubbing the walls around it smooth. And who can ever tell of the running of the waves in the wind?

The waters were the same then. On the surface, visible. But often underground too, their cool nose seeking the sun as they advanced upward through the dark earth.

When we left the forest we came out into an arid landscape, a great bare windswept prairie as far as the eye could see. America, we called it. The southern slope of the plateau is still forested, but on the plateau itself there are hardly any trees. The villages are small and empty: a café-*cum*-tobacconist's serving about three farms, a communal dairy, and a church as tall and sturdy as a fort. Around the church is the graveyard, three centuries of dead, taking up half the village. The only trees are stunted pears, incongruous in the corners of the fields. Nothing grows, because of the chalk. The plain, the fields are lean. It's the chalk. It doesn't retain water.

Because of the sea wind, perhaps, the chalk on the eastern part of the plateau is quite bare. You come to this empty space, then drive down towards marshes crisscrossed by irrigation channels, clay embankments, straight courses of drainage conduits, straight rows of grey-leaved trees seized and stirred by every gust of wind. Then you're there. It's on the the other side of the marsh, on the Seine where it flows between the cliffs. It's at the foot of the cliffs. It's the tanker port of Quillebeuf-sur-Seine.

We look at them: these people, suddenly here in front of us. They come from so far away, an immeasurable distance. And they're at the end of the last voyage, the end of life. It's clear, it's glaring. There, in their humility before death, are these travelers, bestowed upon us.

We don't know how to do without seeing them now, nor how to come to terms with that weariness, that assumed slowness constantly kept from lapsing, that continual miracle. We don't know why we long so to go on seeing them, nor how to retain them within us. Nor can we say what it is. Nor what to call what it is in them that has outlasted time.

What we could do was turn towards that part of the room without seeming to look at anything in particular, as though there wasn't anything there to see and we were deep in our own thoughts.

. . .

The manageress of the Marine went over to the English traveler. She spoke to him in English. Asked him what sort of a voyage they'd had. She called him Captain. *"Glad to see you, Captain."* The Captain answered, *"Yes, we had quite a good trip."* He smiled at her. They knew each other. *"Glad to see you too, Madame."*

It was then we saw that the Captain was dressed as a yachtsman. His cap and white jacket were on a stool beside him.

She, the Captain's wife, looks down at the floor. Her body, hidden before, is now visible. Visible in its mortality. Her body is dressed like a girl's, in the worn-out clothes of youth; on her fingers, the diamonds and gold of her people in Devon. But under the dresses and the skin, death is naked; under the eyes, too, with their pure, shy look. Every so often that look is masked by laughter, which she's immediately scared at having perpetrated. She looks at the Captain to check. And a lost look passes over her face and makes you wonder.

The manageress doesn't come back into the main room. She stays there, leaning against the shelves behind the bar as if having a rest, gazing towards the river, towards the deep pit of blue and black waters.

She's still very good-looking, the manageress of

the Marine, with dark eyes, a porcelain skin, and rosy lips and cheeks. From time to time she looks at the Captain—she avoids looking at the woman who is his wife. She hesitates; she'd like to speak to the Captain again, but she doesn't. The Captain looks as if he'd rather she didn't speak to him, but finally she does. With a sort of bold shyness she says, *"I wanted to tell you* . . . we won't be seeing one another next year. I'm leaving here at the end of this summer. In September . . . *I wanted to tell you."*

The Captain gives a groan, a kind of muffled cry. He says, *"Oh, how sad! How very sad!"* He turns to his wife and exclaims softly, *"She's leaving in September!"* She looks up, shakes her head, and adds her plaint to his: *"Oh no!"*

The manageress has tears in her eyes. She says, "I feel it too . . . You get fond of people without realizing . . . Not necessarily those you see most often."

The Captain says, "Yes, Madame, that's the worst thing about our sort of life. The people we get to know in cafés and restaurants, our friends—we lose them. They move away, or die . . . *Yes, that happens too,* I assure you—they die. It's terrible. Forgive me."

He apologized again. And then all three of them

22

remained silent for a while. Then the Captain asked the manageress what she was going to do when she left the Café de la Marine. She was going to black Africa with her husband. They were taking over a big dance hall and restaurant near Abidjan. It looked promising. They were going to try it out for a year. Her daughter was going to take her place here until they made up their minds. She called her over. It was the girl we'd seen her with in the main room. The young manageress was prettier than her mother, but had the same kind of looks and the same extraordinarily sweet expression in her eyes.

The manageress introduced her daughter to the Captain and his wife. The Captain complimented her on her daughter's looks. The Captain's wife looked up and smiled, and said yes, she was very pretty. The Captain said to the girl, "We're very fond of your mother."

The manageress went back to the main room. When the younger woman was left alone with us by the bar we thought just for a moment that she was different, after all, from her mother. Less subtle, less able to see into people's minds. Not much less, but the things that made the mother's presence so delightful vanished when she did. And that was what happened. Not only did the young manageress speak to the Captain straightaway, as if speaking to the Captain was the easiest thing in the world, but she told him she'd known him all her life, as if he were interested in whether she had or not.

"I used to see you every summer when I was little. When you got back from your trip."

The Captain smiled politely at the young manageress of the Marine. But he did look slightly surprised, while she went on, never doubting she had a perfect right to bore him with the story of her life. It was plain she wanted to know more about the Captain and his wife than her mother did. So there she went, asking the question her mother had never asked:

"So you travel all the time, do you?"

It was an awkward moment for all of us.

A silence falls between the Captain and the young woman. The Captain is surprised, but still smiles affably at the young woman who is his friend the manageress's daughter. And she can't understand why he is surprised. But perhaps at that moment it dawned on her that the voyage these people were on bore no resemblance to the sort of voyage she'd always imagined, and that she shouldn't have asked questions. The woman sitting beside the Captain and gazing down at the floor looked up at her. And suddenly she understood, and blushed with embarrassment.

"I'm sorry."

The Captain smiled at her. We had all been afraid she might ask another question. But she hadn't had time to. The danger point was past.

The Captain said yes, they did travel a lot, they spent a lot of time at sea.

The young manageress, still blushing, still apologetic, said she was very interested in travel. But she'd never been abroad yet, herself.

She didn't go away from the bar, though; she waited. It was suddenly clear she was the sort of person who couldn't give up on anything she'd made up her mind to do. She asked them again where they were going, what part of the world, what seas. But she did so like a child, an obstinate, utterly tactless child. As if she had a right to know. And then she stopped, frightened at her own temerity. The Captain saw this, but he also realized she did have a right to know, and he started to like the young manageress just as he liked her mother. He laughed and said, *"God! How can I possibly tell you?"*

25

The woman gazing down at the floor looked up and laughed too. And so did we.

The Captain told about their latest travels. About Malaysia, Malacca, the Sunda Islands. Had she heard of them? She said she knew the names, Java, Sumatra, Singapore, but of course she couldn't place them exactly. Except perhaps Malacca, because of the Strait, she'd seen that on the map. And wasn't it Malaysia that had so many islands it looked like a continent that had been . . . how could you describe it? . . . blown to pieces in an explosion? The Captain said, *"That's it.* That's exactly what happened. The volcanos in the sea did it. What you see on the map are handfuls of little islands scattered all over the Pacific. The Pacific is a sea full of volcanos and sharks."

The young manageress said everyone in Quillebeuf knew the boat from seeing it go by—a big yacht. The Captain said you had to have a boat that was big and strong for long nonstop trips in the Sea of Oman or the Bay of Bengal, and for going up to Manila or down to Australia.

The Captain said, "So that's the story."

Then he didn't say any more.

The young manageress went and joined the local people at the other end of the bar. And we moved away too, and turned towards the river and its flat blue waters.

Then suddenly we heard the Captain quietly singing a sad tune we didn't recognize, probably some old English foxtrot. And she—she was looking down at the floor again.

I looked at them. And said, "Loving as a form of despair."

You smiled, and I smiled back.

"Running away from everywhere like criminals."

You asked me how deep the small Malaysian seas are. I said they're very deep, a hundred and fifty to two hundred meters, but that in that part of the world there are abysses ten kilometers deep. Probably craters of the volcanos that blew the earlier mainland to pieces. But I thought the deepest abysses were over towards Korea, in the archipelagos that stretch like necklaces almost to the poles. I said that for the people that went on them, those long sea voyages lasting weeks or months were the most extraordinary times of their lives. I said I'd said it before, in my books, and was still saying it, but it was all over and would never come back. Like the age of a thing or a person, that lasts a certain time and never comes back.

.   .   .

We look at them again. They're both gazing down at the floor in a repose that is staggering to see. They're living in the endless voyage of the world, of the sea. It's written on their faces, burned by the wind and the reflection of the sun.

They'd arrived there that evening as if at the finish of a round trip, the end of one voyage and the beginning of the next. And there they were in front of us, yet still deep in the gigantic labor of a great love.

You say something has happened to them. Something external, nothing to do with their story, perhaps an accident, a sudden fear, that has made them stop and wonder what time it was their love was supposed to be lived in. Wasn't it always a time put off until later? A time bereft of hope. The time they were spending now in Quillebeuf, here with us in the Café de la Marine, this vast, empty, idle time, was the one they'd found to live their story in.

"Time."

"Yes."

But perhaps the Captain went to sea in order to hide? After committing a murder? And perhaps she was hiding from some belief, or some fear, which she drowned in whiskey every evening when it got dark?

One sensed they must have lived together through some adversity, and through it have come to know one another so well that they arrived at a common being, in good and ill, crime and innocence. Until the ultimate end in a common death, which so far they'd always avoided, for some reason that didn't matter.

What we didn't know was how far such a love had gone, how deep the divine lie had reached before one or other of the lovers had noticed the difference made by the first betrayal.

The Captain's wife, as she looks down at the floor, is already hidden in death. It gives you a kind of thrill; you feel like catching hold of her hands, her face, and looking into the blue of her eyes, dissolved into a sort of bright spray.

She has looked up at the manageress of the Marine, the one who's going to the Ivory Coast, waved her a kind of farewell, smiled at her. Then looked down at the floor again.

.   .   .

29

Everything lapsed back into silence and immobility. All that was left was the intermittent murmur of conversation in the main room. The tune the Captain was singing quietly. And the tension spread everywhere by the blunder the young manageress had nearly made, about what kind of journey these visitants from the sea were on.

The young manageress stands slightly apart from her mother and the rest. She's looking at the Captain. But she won't come over to him for the rest of the afternoon.

There was a shout, out on the quay.

We went out into the square. Others followed. A few passers-by had already stopped in their tracks. Everyone was looking towards the river.

The bright red ferry, its four arms raised, is crossing the Seine at the same time that a giant tanker is coming in from the sea.

The tanker is heading straight for the ferry. There's about twenty meters between them. They seem not to have seen one another, as if they were prevented from doing so by the difference in size.

The ferry is still moving towards the tanker. The tanker is still bearing down on the ferry—a huge white block, a thing of steel that's suddenly appalling.

The tanker advances so slowly its movement can only be seen in relation to the lines of oil pumps and the rows of trees by the river. Its decks are full of red and blue containers. Yellow too, perhaps.

The ferry has cut across the tanker's bows and disappeared behind it.

The tanker still moves on.

The ferry reappears in the wake of the tanker, heading bold as ever for the landing stage on the right bank. The danger is over. In the square the people who had stopped are walking on again towards the shopping center.

The Koreans, though, hadn't watched the tanker and the ferry cutting across one another. I say, "Look how indifferent they are."

You say they must be used to seeing the Seine ferry taunting the oil juggernauts; they must have been here a long time and grown accustomed to incidents that are only really frightening for visitors.

Suddenly I didn't want to know what you thought any more.

. . .

We went back into the main part of the café with the regular customers, leaving the people at the bar, the English travelers, alone. And it was then I didn't want to know what anybody thought any more. That could happen to me, too. I said there was no point in trying to change the subject. You laughed. It was all one to me. I said I knew Asiatics: they were cruel, they used to amuse themselves on the plain of Kampot by driving their cars over dying dogs. I talked about the flat grey sea of the tropics. And then about Siam again, beyond the mountains. As always when such memories come back to me, they estrange me from you all, from you in particular. They make me feel there's a great distance between us, like the memory of reading about something I could never get over, a passage from one of my books about some part of my youth. And it seemed to me that I must leave you in order to go on writing about Siam and other things that none of you have ever experienced; that I must come back first and foremost, ever and again, to Siam, the sky over the mountains, and other things I used to think about when I should have let them alone, and that now I believed I should have stuck to all my life.

When I thought of what my life had been my whole body was invaded by a sort of numbness, a sadness, and I thought it was because of you. I knew you got worried when I was silent too long, and I used to make an effort to come back closer to you again. But you never did anything to make me do so.

We couldn't possibly lie about the feeling which had united us and probably still did, but which we never mentioned now. We didn't know what it was made of now, what sort of thing it was. We didn't want to know.

You'd let me stay silent a long while, despite your wish to know why I hadn't said anything.

You were looking at the Koreans. No one seemed to have noticed them, though their presence on the terrace of the Hôtel de la Marine was obvious.

Some of them had started playing, running about and chasing each other. More of them had arrived from along the disused path beside the river; they were just the same as the rest—chubby men, prematurely obese. When they ran they bounced along like balls, like big babies. Once again it seemed to me they were going to shut us up in the main room at the Marine and surround the square. I didn't say anything to you. It wasn't fear, just a bearable apprehension. I asked you what you thought: who were these people? A school? A religious brotherhood? Soldiers? Policemen? Airmen? Their age was doubtful too. They might have been anything between fifteen and forty. I said all this was different from anything we'd ever experienced before. For instance, had you noticed there wasn't a single woman among them?—it was so marked as to seem official.

I say it has struck me they might be a club of young eunuchs, though their dress and their behavior seem to suggest they're sailors. This makes you laugh like anything.

I say, "Or perhaps they're the crew of a tanker. But why the sports outfits?"

You look at me hard.

"Why are you the only person in the whole harbor who's afraid of them?"

I smile and say, "I've been told it was probably the colonies—living there as a child—and drink. And that it wasn't anything to worry about, though it would never quite go away."

"You've never talked about it as if it might recur."

"I thought it best I should be the only one to know. To spare you the horror of it."

We both laugh. I say, "It's you I'm afraid of."

This doesn't surprise you much. It makes you want to laugh.

"What aspect of me?"

"You yourself."

. . .

I tell you more about my fear. Try to explain it. I don't succeed. I say it's inside me, I secrete it. It has a paradoxical kind of origin, in biology but at the same time in the imagination. But it does exist, though it hasn't got a language to express itself. When you get down to it, it's a kind of dumb and naked cruelty, directed at myself by myself, in my head, in the solitary confinement of the mind. Cut off. With the occasional break-out in search of reason, probability, and light.

You look at me and give up on me. Look away. Say, "It's just fear, what you've just been talking about. That's what it is, there's no other name for it."

"Una cosa mentale."

You don't answer. Then you say that applies to all sorts of fears.

I say fear is my main point of reference. Causing fear is what constitutes evil. That's what I believe. So do a lot of young people.

I say fear of the dark and fear of God and fear of the dead are bogeys to frighten naughty children with. And that sometimes I see cities as objects of dread, with their thick defensive walls. That's how I see governments, too. And money. And money people. I'm full of echoes of war and of colonial occupa-

35

tion. Sometimes, when I hear orders shouted in German, I have almost a compulsion to kill.

You don't listen to what I'm saying because you're one of those who are afraid but think no one else can understand their fear. You're one of those who never talk about it.

Another reason why you don't listen is that you think there's something in what I say that needs to be understood. And of all the boring things in the world you find explanations the most boring.

You ask me how it is these people frighten me even if they're only a tanker crew done up in sports clothes. I say it's because they don't know they contain the cause of my fear. While they clubbed dogs to death on the plain of Kampot they went on smiling like children. They laughed without a qualm, they enjoyed watching the dying contortions of those fleshless skeletons. I say I can't be like the French of France after a childhood like that.

From time to time we'd look at the couple at the bar. The Captain must have seen us in the mirror. Then we'd look at the river. And then again at the couple. I suddenly stopped talking. You said again it was terrible how much people were still affected by the war.

.　.　.

As usual that made me cry.

We talked about the couple in the bar. We said, She's
so near death, and he'll be left alone. The manageress
went over to them. She served them a black Pilsen
and a bourbon. They said something to one another
and smiled, and looked over at the main room, where
the manageress's daughter was.

You say something must have happened in *their*
youth, too, that determined the course of their lives.
The manageress mentions the time. The Captain tells
his wife, "*It's five o'clock.*" She replies very quietly,
"*Already?*" And asks when they'll be leaving. The
Captain doesn't answer.

The Captain's wife was still waiting, here as everywhere else. You say she must have been waiting all
her life for something like what she's waiting for
here, in the bar. Deliverance from something unbearable. You say, "The sea voyages must be connected
with what you were talking about—some unbearable
impatience."

You also say, "When you look at her, even
through that incredible age, you can see the reasons
why someone might have loved her."

37

"It's different with the Captain."

You agree he's less advanced in years, in eternity.

I point to the Koreans.

"Look at them. Just now I thought they were going to surround the café and exterminate us. As I said, they're very cruel. The most cruel people on earth."

The Koreans are looking the cars, the wheels, the dashboards, the brand marks, the license plates. You follow them with your eyes but you're not interested in them any more. It's me you're looking at.

You ask me, "Why do you have to write that story?"

"I've got nothing else to write. I think it's our story that prevents me writing anything else. But no, that's not true. Our story will never really exist, never be completely written."

You ask me if that's the fate of certain stories.

I don't know. I can't understand what it is you're trying to find out. I say what I do know, that some stories are elusive; they're made up of a series of situations without any link between them. That the most terrible stories are the ones that are never acknowledged, that are lived through without any certainty, ever.

We lower our eyes. Perhaps we would weep if we

looked at one another. You always pay close attention when we talk about writing.

"What prevents me writing is you. And you're unhappy because of it. Because you're not writing either. You're not writing because you know all about that tragic subject—writing, not writing, not being able to write. In your case it's because you're a writer that you're not writing. It can happen."

You give a rather awkward laugh; you're quite moved. I must have been almost crying as I spoke. I don't look at you.

"You know it—what I've just said."

"No, I don't know anything. But I used to know . . . you know how it is . . ." You laugh. "Once you start going on like that it can last forever . . . No, I don't know anything really. I look as if I do, but I don't."

"It could happen to you too. For always, for your whole life. Not to write any more."

"Is that what the fear is, do you think?"

"I don't know. Perhaps a sort of belief that it's forbidden. I look as if I know, too, but I don't know anything either."

. . .

Again we look beyond the words, the moment. We look at the river, the square, the sleeping summer. You ask me, "How did it happen in your case?"

"Sheer idiocy, I expect . . . You have to be an idiot to start thinking it's possible. But that's no answer. How one comes to do it I don't know either, nor why. No one knows why. You start. And then there you are, writing, so you go on. And then there it is, it's happened."

"You were very young. That must have had something to do with it."

"Yes, of course. I was still at school. I must have been about twelve when it happened. And I just let it go on happening . . . until now. But I don't know . . . How it happens at school or not at school, or how it doesn't—I don't know anything about it."

"It's a question of pride."

"With the first book—yes, I expect so. And with some writers—men—that's all there is to it. But after the first book it's not just pride, and it's afterwards that it becomes overwhelming, when it takes possession your whole life long. But it's a question of fear, too, no doubt about it . . . It's as if it protected you from some sort of fear. I mean, it's possible. I don't know."

"Being a writer consists in not knowing."

"No, that's not enough, though it's said so often there must be some truth in it. Writing means, among other things, not knowing what you're doing, being unable to judge it—there's certainly a bit of that in a writer, a blinding light. And then there's the fact that it takes up a great deal of time and calls for a lot of effort—that's an attraction too. It's one of the few occupations that never stop being interesting. We could leave it at that."

We laugh, and then we do leave it at that. You say, "What a life!" Then again you look away and start up again:

"Why did you have to tell me you're going to write that story?"

"Because I tell you everything. If you can't bear it any more you can leave whenever you want—this evening, tomorrow morning. Go back to Paris and move your things out of your room. Go on, go."

The tankers were moving one after the other along the river, coming back from Rouen; the tide was turning. They were tall, empty, and suddenly fragile and light.

"You don't know where to go, that's why you don't want to leave."

"It's not only that. I'm very fond of the apartment, and of my room. I don't see why I should leave my room."

"No. There's no reason why you should."

You didn't say anything for a long while. You'd turned towards the river. Your hair looked very fair in the sun. I thought about it and said, "That's what you are—a man with fair hair. It's the first thing people notice."

You take your time not answering. You're angry. Then you laugh.

"I couldn't care less what you write. That's your business."

"Yes, it is my business. Mine alone. Whatever happens, I'll do as I like."

"Yes, whatever happens. You only do what you've made up your mind to do. It's a defect of yours."

"I have no choice. You leave me no alternative. I don't leave you any either."

"You leave me even less."

"That's true too."

We went on talking like that. And then you said, "What we like best is writing books about one another"—and we laughed.

I said I thought there was a way of getting back

42

to the story. That in my opinion that was what we ought to do. And that according to the resistance it offered we'd know what there was to be done with it.

We weren't looking at anything. You ordered some tea. I said, "Sometimes I think that's all there is. Sometimes I think it's all over. More all over than anyone can imagine. The only sign of life is the thought of death."

"Yes. Death. We can't bear it. But for you it's nothing. Put yourself in my place."

We laugh again at death. We look at the bridge at Tancarville, the pink above the sea.

You said, "We'll have been to Quillebeuf often this summer."

"Yes. Do you know why we like it so much? I don't."

"I know up to a point, but to know entirely is impossible."

"Yes. It's something there staring you in the face, but it blinds you so that you can't see it."

Suddenly you were looking at the square, and you said, "The Koreans have gone."

The square was empty again, except for two little

boys on bikes who'd also come from along the disused path. The shadow had reached the other bank of the river. Part of the sky, to the north, had turned leaden: it wasn't evening yet, but a storm was crossing the sky over the bay, very high and slow. It got very dark: people said it was because of the impending storm. And then instead, beneath the leaden sky, it was bright sunlight again. All the oil installations, with their steel and their bright surfaces, sparkled.

For a few seconds a kind of mystery reigned. We tried to find the sun.

It was very low in the clear part of the sky, lighting up the countryside and harbor underneath the storm. The estuary was lit up right down to the sea. And the stormy sky was trapped in the wave of light. The storm stayed where it was, not spreading over the sky, not breaking, but dark and unchanging, a cope of black stone. We went on looking.

We looked at the white rail along the banks of the Seine: it was ridiculously inadequate for its purpose, which was to keep people out of the river. I said that for me the white of the rail beside the water was an unfathomable problem. You said the river was criss-crossed and held in place by the grid of the rail—the blue-black of the water by the milky white—just as the blue was held in place by the white in Nicolas de Staël's last paintings.

We went back into the bar, ordered some long drinks, and looked at the people. The local people, the jokesters. The manageress. And her terrible and charming daughter. And at them, the English travelers. I talked some more about the Asiatics. I said they were cruel, and gamblers and thieves and hypocrites and madmen, and I had vivid memories of the animals in Indochina, all gaunt and mangy as in southern Spain and black Africa. I said the memories of animals were the most painful of all, because young children can't bear to see animals suffer; they'd rather see people die than dogs and elephants and deer and tigers and monkeys.

While I'm talking to you I'm looking at the two glasses standing next to ours on the bar. In one is the strong beer, the black Pilsen, and in the other the double bourbon *on the rocks,* the same as a little while ago, only now the glasses are full. They must have been refilled while we were outside.

I turned to you and whispered the name of an American writer. Dead. Committed suicide. You nodded. Yes, that was it.

. . .

45

Now the travelers seem to be talking. They exchange bits of sentences at long intervals, occasionally just the odd word. But gradually we begin to understand what they're talking about.

"What a shame . . . I was longing to go home."

"Don't think about it, dear . . . Please."

"Oh dear, I'm so tired. Exhausted . . . Such a pity. Especially now, just when . . ."

"Yes, yes, my dear. Don't think about it. There's nothing to be done."

"No . . . I'm not . . . It's just that . . ."

"No, don't. Please . . ."

"All right, darling . . . You're so sweet . . . Do forgive me."

The boat they were traveling on, that's what they were talking about. It must have been in some little port on the Seine, waiting for them. And for various landing and residence permits. Probably they couldn't sail right away because they didn't have all the papers they needed to leave France and enter England. That could have been it. Whether the permits were for themselves or the boat, we couldn't tell. They must often have forgotten things, including applying for permits. She wanted to go ahead without them, she said you could enter England whenever you liked if you were English. But he didn't agree. It was as if some last wish had come upon her all of a sudden. But he seemed not to realize this yet. She wanted to get away from France, and to get away now, this evening.

The immensity of their love becomes very clear as they lapse into restrained anger or alcoholic stupor. There's obviously some difficulty between them this evening that we can't make out. They look at each other, slightly annoyed. And pained.

Then they look down at the floor, or into the void, at the people going by in the square or the comings and goings of the red ferry.

Then they look at one another again with newly dawning love.

You look at the river. The setting sun is shining right inside the café. It's in your laughing eyes. You say, "They're the longest-distance travelers in the world. They're living the world's longest journey."

The words delight you.

I say they must have a room in Venice and call in there like all the travelers in the world returning to their native country. And they must be stopping at

47

Quillebeuf on their way back to England. They probably can't do otherwise. Whereabouts in England? We don't know.

That year the dates must have been the ones they'd planned.

That year they were punctual; it was time that was late.

I smile at you and say, "It's June, the month for going home."

The manageress of the Marine comes back into the bar and speaks to the Captain again. She too says June is a good month for coming back to Europe. And this year there's going to be a good summer. She asks him if they're going away again. She can always ask the Captain questions. Even forbidden questions, the ones that are bound to upset him. But those she never asks. *"Are you going away again, Captain?"* The Captain says it depends on his wife. *"Sometimes she wants to go, sometimes she doesn't . . . It's a long way, you see, a very long way indeed . . . "* He says this is bound to be one of their last long trips. There may be other, shorter ones, but it's not certain.

Then the Captain is silent.

She looks down at the floor again, ashamed of having to die.

．　．　．

The Captain shuts his eyes. He's trying to remember
the French words he must have known once. But
he's forgotten them. He says, *"She's just like a child
. . . "* Then he stops. He looks to see if the manageress
is listening. She's gone. He goes on for the benefit of
the rest of us. Sometimes she wants to go back to
England. Sometimes she can't bear to hear England
mentioned. It's very near—the Isle of Wight, you can
touch it with your hand. One night's voyage and
you're there. It's there . . . The Captain's voice is
halting and low. It's there that the family house is.
Yes. It's not us he's talking to, it's to the little iguana.
The caretaker is still there. Yes. You wonder what he
can be taking care of, but he's still there anyway. The
first caretaker stayed on until he was terribly old,
almost a hundred. He died there. And after that there
was a very young one who left after three or four
years. Now there's a third one who's just normally
old. Apart from that, everyone's dead now, the neigh-
bors, the other relatives. He and she are the only
ones left now, they and the caretaker. There are a few
pieces of furniture still, things that wouldn't go into
the moving vans and haven't been stolen. But the
house is still there, and the famous wood by the sea.
The little iguana raises her eyelids, listening to the

string of facts. Her father was against their marriage. So they waited until he died. The mother died first, and then the father. They had to wait a long time. *Yes.* Ten years. He, the Captain, had been taken on to look after the boat. He was twenty-two at the time. She was twenty-six then, and beautiful . . . *my God . . . so amusing . . . so witty . . . my God . . . my God . . . how far away it all seems . . .* When the father died, he was thirty-two and she was thirty-six, the sole heiress. They went away immediately after the wedding. She insisted. *Yes.* So there it is. He stops. Looks at her. She turns very slightly towards him. He speaks a little louder.

He knows she's listening to the story. Every evening, a little, he has to speak for her, in her stead.

I say he can never really have understood the girl from the Isle of Wight. The woman he has loved. And she must have known it.

I say he must have been aware of her occasional fits of revulsion against the boat, against travel, even if she didn't talk about them. But he just put it down to ill-humor, and said it happened at the end of every trip. But she was increasingly convinced that in her travels she'd forgotten all about the house, what the drawing room was like, and her bedroom, and the path down to the sea; the garden, and the wood by the sea, and the eucalyptus trees that were planted the day she was born. And she even wanted to know about the apartment over the boathouse. That was why she wanted to go back—to see, to check. The Captain didn't want to hear about all that. He let her talk, but didn't listen. He wasn't interested in all the ins and outs; he refused to enter into the details of her moods.

To tell the truth, the Captain must have feared the worst every time they came back to this part of the world—must have been afraid it might be the last time, that it might all be over.

Now we know. What they're talking about has to do with the early years of their love. They used to call in for an hour at the house on the Isle of Wight. She'd look at the grounds and at some of the rooms—often without going in, just from the door. And then, before dusk, she'd want to leave—to escape before it gets dark, she used to say. They'd got into the habit of staying at a certain hotel in Newport. She was always glad to see the town again. But it wouldn't be many mornings before she'd say, in the hotel bedroom, that she wasn't going back to sea again, that it was all over, completely, forever.

This evening the Captain is frightened. This time,

she doesn't say why, she wants to go and sleep in the house on the Isle of Wight. He doesn't want to let her, he thinks it's far-fetched and unreasonable. He thinks it's almost improper of her to insist like that, she who's usually so polite and charming. *"She carries things to extremes,"* he says. *"She goes too far. She's always changing her mind."*

She isn't interested in what he says about her.

It was probably during the ten years they had to wait for her parents to die that something happened to make them decide to spend the time their love lasted traveling on the sea. So as to do nothing with their love and yet at the same time preserve it.

The Captain was her first lover. It had happened soon after he was taken on to look after the boat.

They tried to stop loving one another, but they couldn't. When they saw it was impossible, it was she who told her parents they wanted to get married. The parents refused to allow it. No. Not as long as we're alive. She'd lived with them all her life. She could never have imagined they'd stand in the way of their daughter's happiness. That they'd actually be the cause of her unhappiness, building it up day after day, stone by stone.

The parents never gave in. And they never regretted it. Not even on their deathbeds. Neither did the children—they never gave in, and they never regretted it.

If the Captain wasn't dismissed it was because she, their daughter, would have gone with him wherever he went. They knew their daughter, they knew she'd have killed herself if she was deprived of her lover. The father, especially, knew their daughter as well as it's possible to know another human being. His knowledge of her derived from his knowledge of his wife, the mother of his child; it was part of it. They were both women who could never be parted from their lover's body, day or night, mentally or physically. And the dependence of the women meant that the men couldn't part from them either. The father knew the relationship between their daughter and the Captain was like that. He was sure his decision to keep them there those ten long years was partly to save them from their own folly. And not only did the parents keep the Captain on in his job, they also paid him an allowance so that they could both live in the apartment in the grounds of the house which went with the job. So they could still see their daughter occasionally as she walked along the quays or the beach, her face turned towards the sea.

.   .   .

That lasted ten years.

So it was in the two rooms over the boathouse that they spent those ten years.

It was there they started to drink, and to play cards with the servants from the houses nearby and the summer campers. Gradually she stopped going to church and gave up the English Protestantism she'd been brought up in.

But apart from that, all her feelings remained the same.

She still loved her father and mother very much. She and the Captain soon stopped bearing them any sort of grudge. Neither of them ever mentioned what had happened. The crime the parents had committed was so terrible it absolved them: it was as if they'd been its victims too. They hadn't been able to understand where their daughter's real happiness lay, and the best thing to do was forget it. The whole island knew about it, and everyone did the same: they forgot it. They said the parents had paid for what they'd done, in suffering. But their daughter did bear a grudge against fate, and the upsetting of what she'd believed was life's divine order. While he, the Captain, thought one should never bear a grudge against anyone for anything.

. . . .

One day, when she'd been living with the Captain in the apartment over the boathouse for four years, she wrote some poems. It wasn't the first time. She'd always written before, but after she met the Captain she didn't write anything for some years. And then suddenly she started again.

It lasted a year.

She wrote poems. Fifteen poems.

One of them was published in a literary magazine in Newport.

She told the Captain that she put all her passion for him into her poems, and at the same time all the despair of every living creature.

But the Captain thought she didn't put what she said she put into her poems. He didn't know what she really put into them. That was the Captain's position as regards his wife's poems.

The Captain suffered. Suffered tortures. As if she'd betrayed him, as if she'd led another life at the same time as the one he thought she'd been living in the apartment over the boathouse. A life that was secret, hidden, incomprehensible, perhaps even shameful, and more painful to him than if she'd been unfaithful with her body. The body that was the one thing in the world for which, before the poems, he'd probably have killed her if she'd given it to another man.

. . .

Once he spoke to her about it, about how the poems made him suffer because he couldn't understand them. She must have misunderstood his confession. She said if they made him suffer it probably meant he'd begun to understand them.

And then once, on the brink of despair, the Captain went to talk to her father. He'd never stopped seeing her parents. He visited them occasionally in their luxurious villa. He and the father had always had a great respect for one another. The father never asked after his daughter, but he knew the Captain came to give them news about her, which he did at length every time. While the Captain was there they also used to talk about the grounds, repairs to the house, their health, and local doings.

On this occasion the Captain told the father how anxious and upset he was about the poems. And the father seemed pleased. A strange smile appeared on his face, and remained on it all the time the Captain was there. The father made no reference to the Captain's suffering and anxiety. He just asked him to copy the poems and bring them to him. The Captain promised.

He kept his promise without telling her. He took all the poems there were in the black folder on the chest of drawers in the bedroom, copied them carefully, and took them to her father.

The father read them in front of him. Then read them again. And wept. He didn't say a word, except to apologize for crying. For joy, he said. For crying for joy. He said he'd been expecting something like this to happen ever since his daughter was a very little girl.

The Captain went home. And found himself alone again.

It was soon after that that the poem was published in a literary magazine in Newport.

She wondered mildly how it could possibly have happened. Then, strangely, she let the matter drop. Bowed to the mystery of circumstance. After all, the immanence of a poem, the way it entered into people's minds, was just as mysterious. She believed poems written in one country soon spread to others, breaking down by their own mere existence and self-evidence the barriers of seas, skies, continents, political systems, and prejudice. She was one of those who incline to believe the same poem is written everywhere, but in different forms. That there's only one poem to be sought for through every language and all civilizations.

At that point—she'd written nineteen poems, autumn had gone by—she stopped.

And then there came a terrible time for them.

She lost a little girl at birth in a nursing home in Newport. She wanted to die. She wanted to go away. Steal her father's boat and go away. She shouted unintelligible words during the night, called for help from people with unfamiliar names. She shrieked out how much she loved her father and mother, and how much she hated them. Then she stopped, and only wept for days and nights on end. And then that ceased too, like the poems. She had asked the Captain to look at their dead little girl so that he could tell her parents what she was like, and ask them if they noted any resemblance to her. The Captain had done as she asked. He'd gone to see the parents and described to them the pale eyes, huge and grey, and the black Irish hair.

Summer returned, and so did her reason. One morning she woke up almost normal again, and the Captain recognized her. And then this is what happened:

Although she didn't write any more poems all that summer and autumn, one day in January she started

again. It was a poem about the light there is sometimes, on certain cold dark winter afternoons. She
didn't tell the Captain.

Then one day when she'd gone out and the Captain
was waiting for her to come home, he saw the poem
just by chance. It hadn't been tucked all the way into
the black folder on the chest of drawers in their
bedroom; a white sheet of paper was sticking out. The
Captain tried to pull it straight and the page came
away in his hand. And there the poem was in front
of him, exposed like a crime. This was after the long
period in which she hadn't written anything, the
period after the death of their little girl that terrible
night in Newport.

And there the Captain had been, thinking her
youthful whims and fancies were over.

He felt as if he'd been stabbed by the truth. As if
he'd taken her for someone else and been living with
a stranger. There was nothing in the poem about the
dead child or about him. No mention of their life
together, their love, their happiness.

It was the coldest day of that winter, the end of
January. Yes, it was six months after he'd thought
she'd given up all that rubbish.

The poem wasn't finished. That was why it wasn't
put right away inside the black folder. It was an

unfinished poem that stopped in the middle. But the beginning was there in its final form, written out more firmly than the rest. The middle of the poem, with its variants, took up half the page. It was full of cross-outs. At first it was about the terrible light of certain winter afternoons. And the light it spoke of was just like the light that same day: a bloody glare of yellowish mauve that left its stain on the gardens of all the houses on the island, on the wintry horizons, on the boats held fast in the frozen docks. It was as if she'd written the poem that very afternoon.

The poem seemed to have been written deliberately to hurt the Captain. Moreover, it completely ignored him. He was in agony. He tried again to think what he could have done to make her consider him so insignificant—and what he should have done so as to be mentioned, however slightly and indirectly. And then he stumbled on the, to him, appalling truth: that in her universe he never had existed, and never would.

The Captain read the poem again, both the part with the cross-outs and the part that was free of alterations. The latter seemed even more alien than the passages she'd had doubts about. In the altered parts she said that on certain winter afternoons the slanting rays of the sun were as oppressive as the sound of cathedral organs.

In the unaltered parts she said the wounds inflicted on us by these swords of the sun were dealt by heaven. They left no visible trace, no scar either on our flesh or in our thoughts. They neither wounded nor consoled. It was a matter of something else. Somewhere else. Far away from where we might have thought. The wounds did not herald or confirm anything that could be taught. What they did was produce a new perception, an inner difference at the heart of meaning.

Towards the end the writing became uncertain and hard to decipher. It said, or almost said, that the inner difference was reached through, and was in a way the mark of, supreme despair. After that the poem trailed off in a flight through the last valleys before the heights, the cold summer night, and a vision of death.

The Captain threw the poem into the stove. To end his suffering—that's what he told himself. Then he waited for he knew not what, in the room with the stove that she had to go through to get to the bedroom. And he stopped suffering for a while as he waited for her return.

But in the respite that followed the poem's disappearance, another image of his wife occurred to the Captain. It was then, after the poem had been destroyed, that he realized what he'd done, and was afraid.

It was through his wife's ignorance about him that he realized her innocence. Suddenly he saw her once more as unaware of her power over him. Her innocence was such that she'd written the poems without realizing that their worth derived from their very obscurity. She was a child who had to be protected against herself, against an obscurity so clear to her that she took it for her own nature.

She came back from a walk through the little roads around the parents' house. She said it was exceptionally, frighteningly cold out. Then they had a cup of tea. And she went into the bedroom. She didn't close the door. It must have taken her a moment to notice the poem wasn't there. She looked for it, then asked the Captain if he'd seen a sheet of paper with writing on it that had been left on top of the chest of drawers.

He said he hadn't.

She spent part of the evening and night trying to find it. She took the drawers out of the chest of drawers and emptied them. He stayed in the dining room while she searched. Every so often he asked her if she'd found it. She said no. Finally she wrenched at the top two drawers of the chest of drawers and broke them, trying to make sure the poem hadn't fallen down behind them. But there was nothing there. Then she came into the room where the Captain was, sat down facing him, and looked at him:

"I've looked everywhere. I won't find it. I give up. It was a different kind of poem," she added. "I'd have liked to show it to you. But only because I show you everything I write, not because I think you'd have liked it. In fact, I think it would have made you afraid for me, made you think my head's not better yet from the death of our little girl. So perhaps it's all for the best."

The Captain looked at his wife and said yes, he probably wouldn't have understood that poem any more than he had the others.

She said she wished she could have finished it, but it was best not to think about it. They were both silent. Then they went to bed. It was cold, he held her close to keep her warm, he told her he loved her more than anything in the world, and she said she knew.

You listened to the story. You too said what had happened between them was good. You said you'd recognized the poem and the winter light. And the poem's sudden rush towards the unintelligibility of truth.

For a long time we didn't say anything.

Then we talked about all the time that had gone by between that winter day and this moment, this evening, in this French harbor.

It must have been after the loss of the poem that she thought of sea travel, decided to waste her life on the sea, to do nothing else with the poems or with love but waste them on the sea.

After that there couldn't have been a question of anything else between them, nor any other problem or any other way of solving it, except through the mere passage of time. All other uses for their love were rejected. Happiness was rejected. Writing was banished.

It was difficult for us to see them now as we'd seen them for the first time a little while ago. We were too close to them—stiflingly close. We needed to draw away a little to see them together and take them away with us. We moved away from that end of the bar. You came close to me.

. . .

The Koreans hadn't come back. The square was still empty. Night had begun to fall. The cliffs looked different. Barer, not so white.

From a distance we see them in such a way we'll never forget them. But it's difficult to hear what they're saying—almost impossible. We can make out the beginning of the sentences and some odd words. But that's all. Four black Pilsens the Captain's had, and she's had three bourbons. They don't quite know themselves what they're talking about. Probably everything at once. They start talking to one another, and then forget. Then they stop. They talk to themselves. They complain. He sometimes weeps a little. There's no point in listening to what they're saying. You can tell it's still about the boat, and the darkness engulfing the wild valley. The river and its deserted banks. This region, this country that offers no help to ships in distress or to wayfarers over the face of the earth. Their attachment to the boat has come to be like a religion keeping them together on the sea, and without it they might have been lost to each other forever.

We looked at them for a long while. They paid no attention to anything or anyone. We could have looked at them all night without their noticing or feeling anything. They were so alone in the world, they'd forgotten what solitude was.

Their physical presence has now invaded the main room of the Café de la Marine. People look at them in spite of them and in spite of themselves. You wonder how such innocence is possible. It sustains them and protects them like a garment.

They fall silent. They forget, go to sleep, wake up. And then they start talking again.

She was always the one who spoke first. Then he'd answer her straightaway, she'd take an enormously long time to say another sentence or even another word, and he would be disheartened. That was how it went.

What with their preoccupation about the boat, and the thing the Captain was so afraid of, not knowing whether she'd made up her mind about it or not, they were much more cut off from other people than by the mere fact of speaking a foreign language.

She felt very lonely, her head full of the boat. Lonelier than he was. She drank the double bourbon very, very slowly. It was he who stopped her from drinking more. He knocked back his beer, the black Pilsen, as if it was water. But he watched her whenever she picked up the glass of bourbon. After one sip he'd put his hand on hers and she'd stop. Put the glass down again.

The manageress said the crew from their boat would come and fetch them when it was dark and take them back on board. There was nothing to worry about.

But she couldn't face staying there another night, she just couldn't. But now it was he, not she, who was in charge of the boat, and the crew who were coming were under his orders and only did as he told them. Before, she must have taken charge sometimes too. She used to take the helm in the calm waters along the coast; she enjoyed that. But now neither he nor the crew would trust her. No one said anything, but she knew she wasn't strong enough now. With money it was different. At the beginning he'd said he would never have anything to do with it, it belonged to her. So she had taken care of the money, and that had gone on a long time, years and years. Now she was still supposed to check the accounts, but she only did it now and again because it sent her to sleep.

What she liked best was dozing on deck.

There was one thing that seemed rather a pity:

because of the difference in their origins the Captain treated her with slightly exaggerated deference, but he did so rather too often, and it got on her nerves. But the Captain was proud of his wife's pedigree, which according to him was so ancient and so untainted that some of her ancestors were supposed to have tombs in English cathedrals.

In the bar. The Captain. He keeps his eye lowered for a long time, then suddenly looks at her as you might look at a moving and mysterious landscape—an empty sky or ocean.

The problem must have been the time they had left to live. How not to shorten it by a single day, a single hour, a single place, a single sentence.

You say, "Do they seem so unreal because their traveling, which would otherwise have been perfect, took place in a void?"

The Captain. He is very much slowed down by his passion for her, still as secret as it was the first summer. He's also slowed down by the thickening of his blood, a slackening of the flow that's due to alcohol.

. . .

The manageress came and spoke to the Captain again. She asked him in a low voice, again in English, about a dog. *"Captain, tell me . . . What happened to your little black dog?"* The Captain said it was dead. *"An accident . . . Yes . . . a month ago . . . It's very sad for her."* He nodded towards her, sitting looking at the floor. She'd heard what the manageress said. She was ashamed because of the dead dog.

I look at her. The thought goes through my mind that I could have picked up her bourbon and drunk it myself. Either she wouldn't have noticed, or else she'd have seen and thought it quite natural, and just sat half asleep on the barstool and watched me, a faint smile on her lips. The Captain might have noticed more, for both of them. He might have smiled at me first, and then said, "Thank you for drinking it for her. It does her so much harm, it's terrible. *It's difficult to explain . . .*" He might have wept.

But I only thought of all that afterwards, when it was already too late. I don't know why I'd have done such a thing, anyway—it would have been dangerous for me. Perhaps out of desire for that salty skin, for the smell of her chapped and sea-smelling lips on the glass.

But I didn't pick up the glass. I didn't have a sip of bourbon and a taste of ship's varnish in my mouth, nor a burst of alcoholic violence inside me. Nor a sunlike glow coursing through my body.

The Captain is always looking at her; but it's different with her—she no longer looks at anyone. He never really takes his eyes off her. He still loves her with all his sexual strength. But it's different with her— she's already otherwise engaged, partly in death, partly in laughter, and partly in heaven knows what. So she hasn't the strength left to choose a man. But every night she lets him do as he likes. Rummage as much as he pleases inside her, and get orgasms with pin-ups from the islands. He buys the magazines in the harbor at Singapore.

When he looked away it was only to look down at the floor and then quickly back at her, to check that she was still safe on her stool, laughing softly at something or other, some image, or calling the dead dog with endearments that bring tears to his eyes. *My little one . . . little Brownie . . .*

Someday, he knew it couldn't be long now, he would turn to her and find she'd fallen down on the floor. *Darling . . . Darling . . .*

He knew it was coming closer, like an invisible

landfall in the darkness of the oceans. *Darling . . . My poor little girl . . .*

The light of the setting sun is falling on the other bank of the river. But the red reflection reaches the main room of the Café de la Marine. It moves over the walls, the mirror. And over the two motionless figures that don't look at anything, either you or the sun.

Suddenly the Captain's whole body is swept by despair. He sits up, he breathes fast, then he slumps down again. It was very brief, but it leaves him exhausted. He looks at *the French* with dislike. As if he's fed up with them. He groans. What are the French to him? He's given up trying to take an interest, given up listening to what they're saying as they stand around the bar. He feels awkward among them, trussed up. And the only person who sees him is her, the iguana. She has turned her head towards him, opened her eyes, looked at him: *"What's the matter?"*

It was scarcely audible. Then she looked down at the floor again. The tone had been faintly chiding, as with Brownie. Then she was off again in the love that must now encompass all the affections—for departed dogs, for the things of childhood and family—and all the passions, especially guiltless ones. *My God* . . . all those summers lost like blood . . . and the dead child . . . And the poems . . . the overwhelming grief . . . the light tinged with blood, into whose realms she entered alone, in innocence and evil. *My God,* all that innocence, and all that evil around it. The mere thought . . . All the dangers . . . The Captain's heart still quaked at the memory of life.

The setting sun climbs higher up the walls. It's no longer on the mirror.

Above the corridor formed by the river the gulls veer wildly in the wind. Beneath their wings, the whiteness of the cliffs.

I say, "He doesn't want her to die. In a way he's forbidden her to, because he doesn't want her death in his life—no, he won't allow it, ever."

It was natural that he should try to find a meaning for his own life in terms of hers. She'd lived with him on the boat for so long, he couldn't remember how many years.

Sometimes he must have wondered how he'd survived all the problems that had arisen because of her, because of her awkward character, and also the difference in their birth. The Captain blamed that for

72

everything he hadn't been able to understand about her: her reading, her madness, and also her aberrations, those fearful poems. He was sure she didn't think about them any more, and he thanked God for it. The Captain had never been able to forget the discrepancy in their origins: he saw it as a vast and permanent difference between them. He must have suffered vicariously for her having married beneath her, and he must think he was suffering for it still. But who knows? Perhaps he was thinking about it for the first time during their enforced stay in this little harbor on the Seine. The French people around the bar stared at her so, that could have given him the idea. He hadn't been able to talk to her about it; she refused. At first it had amused her. Later it hadn't.

Every so often the Captain gives us a faint smile and indicates her with a flicker of the eyes. But almost imperceptibly. It's very faint, almost nothing, scarcely a glance or the twitch of a finger. *"Look at her . . . She's my wife . . .* How do you say it in French? *She's a character . . . Yes . . ."* He laughs. *"But she doesn't know what she wants."*

No.

He stops.

There's no point.

He's given up trying to hear what people are whispering around the bar. It's useless. And it only adds to the pain.

From time to time she must spin him a yarn, tell him she'd like to go around the world again, see the Strait of Malacca, Ismailia, the quays beside the Canal. And perhaps he's said it's impossible, those days are over forever, boats are dangerous for a person of her age—always in the same even tone and with the same astounding gentleness he always used with her. She would have acquiesced. Or that's what it would have looked like. But heaven knows what she really thought.

Time went by around them. So much of it had already flowed by, they must have forgotten sometimes how far they'd got to. You say, "Drink will blur things when the time comes. Drink and dementia."

But perhaps not, perhaps we were wrong. Perhaps it was every night, wherever they were, that she wanted to see Newport and the island again. Perhaps every evening of every day, especially in the last few years, with the languishing gentleness, the incredible tact of the English, she'd asked to be allowed to die.

Some customers left. Others arrived.

. . .

Dusk. The light of dusk everywhere. The streets, the ships in the harbor. The rooms in the Café de la Marine. A gold, a pink and gold light that's reflected back from the bright surfaces of the tanker port on the other side of the river.

For a long while the couple, the alcoholics at the bar, don't look at the lights or the harbor; they're not interested. And then they wake up.

Suddenly the Captain points to the people. The river. The square. The sky. His hand describes a kind of circle, and under his breath he reviles them all— the people, the gods, the river, and the sky.

The Captain reviles them. He doesn't want to see anything anymore, not the summer, nor this country nor this weather nor these people. She's the only one he wants to see in the whole world. *My darling.*

It's too big for them now, a summer evening, too far from the river, too far from the boat. It's become impossible. They must give it all up now in earnest— the sea bathing, the walks in the forest, the standing around in bars. They must just give up. She's too tired now, she hasn't the strength to keep going back and forth, she hasn't the strength to stand up to things. Anyway, she hasn't got any shoes left. The ones she has got she's had for ten years, they're finished. The kind of shoes she likes, the kind she's always worn, gradually, without their noticing, got to be hard to find. Now they're not to be had at all. Before the succession of ordinary factory shoes they'd found in the shops during the last ten years, she'd had some made to measure in Southampton—they were the best she'd had in her whole life. They reminded her of the machine-made kind she liked. But the place in Southampton had gone bankrupt. So there it was. They could have had others made to measure some-where else, of course, but where would they have waited for the wretched things? A year it took to make them. Where could they have waited? Clothes were another thing, but in the long run it all boiled down to the same—nothing fitted her any more, and she positively refused to go into a shop. So? So what? So nothing. That's how it was now. Anyhow, new shoes would hurt her feet—they've grown very sensi-tive with age. She wears little children's sandals now. The Captain calms down. He smiles.

It's different for him, says the Captain. He's still strong, and he's got plenty of shoes. The trouble with him is that without her he doesn't want to go on living. He wants her with him everywhere, and would even if he lived in Buckingham Palace.

The little iguana, looking down at the floor, laughs

like anything. She says something only he hears and that makes him laugh too, some joke between them. We join in. You bend over me and laugh into my hair.

Then she starts to moan again, about Brownie, who jumped off the boat and was drowned.

The Captain stops laughing.

He looks at the bundle of old clothes and hair dyed and dyed again, the broken nails and the teeth chipped from all the times she's fallen down on the boat at night, trying to find where he's put the whiskey. Then he turns his head away and doesn't look any more.

They weren't comfortable on barstools, but they managed to sit on them three hours a day, either in the bar on the ship or in the bars on the islands, out there in the damp heat and beneath the grey sky of the tropics.

You, the man with laughing eyes, said, "She wants to die. *That's the point.* Another of her whims."

I agreed it probably was a whim, to want to die like that, when she wasn't ill, when in fact she was happy.

She mumbled something about the dog again, then said quite clearly she thought about him more and more: "*I'm always thinking of him . . . poor little boy.*"

She was talking to the Captain. But the Captain shouted at her to leave it alone. She didn't say anything after that.

You say it's also because she loved the Captain so much that she sometimes wanted to leave him.

The Captain looks at us. He knows when we're talking about his wife. He smiles, he's shy. The Frenchwoman nods to him. Asks in a whisper what his wife's name is, her Christian name. The Captain, also in a whisper, tells her—apparently with some apprehension. She has heard. She raises her head and looks. She questions him very softly: *"What's the matter?"* He nods towards the Frenchwoman. *"Nothing . . . This lady wants to know your name . . ."*

She looks at the woman who asked her name. She gives a sharp little mocking laugh. At the idea of still being given a name. Then she's looking down at the floor again.

You're still talking about the woman at the bar, the Captain's wife.

You say she's very perceptive.

.   .   .

Some cars drive away from the square, others arrive. People come into the café, go into the main room; we can hear them ordering their evening drinks.

I say, "What never came back is her belief in God."

The father died without knowing anything about the poem on winter light.

He'd had the nineteen other poems published. First in a London literary review and then in a slim volume, under her maiden name. She had never known about it. The Captain thought she never would. That it was too late.

The new caretaker at the house had told the Captain some mail had come for her, *the lady,* and he'd returned it to the publisher in London, as the father had asked him to do before he died. The caretaker also said some young men had come to see her, *the lady,* during the first year after the book was published. And a few more came every year. Every year there were new ones.

This caretaker had been taken on by the father just before he died: he'd talked to him mostly about his daughter.

When the Lady came she never asked any questions, either. One day the caretaker asked the Captain why everyone made such a mystery about the Lady's book. The Captain said it was because she wrote the poems when she was young, she hadn't written any since, and she was no longer interested in them.

The caretaker had a press copy of the book, sent by mistake when it was reprinted. He'd read the nineteen poems. He told the Captain he found them too difficult. He didn't understand them. But he found them very impressive and beautiful. The Captain didn't answer. The young caretaker instinctively hid the book in his room over the boathouse.

The poems were translated in two or three European countries. But they hadn't yet got as far as where she and the Captain went, among the islands in the Malaysian seas.

One summer during their annual visit, the bold young caretaker took advantage of the Captain's momentary absence—he must have been out in the grounds inspecting the plants—to show the Lady the book of poems. At first she didn't understand; then she asked how long ago it was published.

"Four years."

She was still young then, too. She was beautiful. Her eyes were large and grey and very deep. She was tanned by the sun, and wearing a white and blue summer dress. She looked at the book in bewilderment. She didn't hold out her hand. She didn't take it. As if, for some reasons that escaped him, she ought not to.

"How did it happen?"

"Through your father. He saw to it all."

She didn't understand: "How do you mean, my father? He didn't know anything about them."

The caretaker knew: the Captain had taken the poems to the father to have them published.

The Lady smiles: *"The Captain's so good to me."* She looks at the caretaker, the same age as she is and plainly adoring her. She smiles, lowers her voice, and asks, "How many poems?"

"Nineteen."

She thinks. She hesitates. Then asks, "Is there one about winter afternoons?"

The caretaker tries to think: "No. I don't think so. Is that the title?"

"Yes. It would have been. Yes, I'm sure."

The caretaker repeats, "Winter afternoons."

She looks at him intently. He says, "No. It isn't there."

She repeats after him that it isn't there.

She looks out into the grounds. Then at the caretaker, who's watching her. She says, "I wasn't sure . . ."

"What do you mean?"

"I remember I thought I'd put it down on a chest of drawers. I was sure—you know how it is—sure I'd put it down under a black notebook. Then I went out for a walk, and when I came back it wasn't there. I never found it again."

He says, "Are you sure you wrote it?"

"Why, do you think I only imagined it?"

"I don't know. Do you remember what you wanted to write about?"

"The rays of the sun, in winter. They creep in wherever they can, through the smallest cracks in the vaulting, the little openings the builders left in the nave so that the light could enter the cathedral and reach down to the pitch-dark of its floor. In winter the sun is a bloody, yellowish mauve . . . I said the rays of the sun wounded like heavenly swords, piercing the heart . . . but without leaving any scar, any trace, except . . . except . . . I forget, and yet it was the most important thing of all. Except . . . But . . ."

Then, after a pause, all in one breath:

"But internal difference where the meanings are."

She says, "I can't remember any more. I hadn't started writing the rest of the poem."

They both lower their eyes. He says, "Perhaps you knew so clearly what you wanted to write . . . that you thought you'd actually written it."

She doesn't answer.

He repeats the words:

"But internal difference where the meanings are."

She doesn't move. She says, "I can't help thinking I did write it. I seem to remember when it happened. If I shut my eyes I can still feel the effort I was making to write fast, and yet not leave anything out. The paper slipped, and I caught at it with my other hand and tore it . . . What do you think?"

He lowers his eyes and says, "I don't think you did write it . . . The sort of difficulty you talk about often happens in dreams . . . you keep losing everything . . . or something's missing."

She starts to weep without realizing it.

"It's unthinkable . . . You didn't write it."

He weeps too. At having to lie.

She sinks back in her chair and starts to tremble, to be afraid of everything she sees in this little sitting room on the second floor. She says, "I'm sorry . . . It's the first time anyone has ever talked to me about what I write."

He comes over and breathes on her hands to warm them.

And then it all stops, the fear, the cold, as for a long moment her eyelids are pressed down over her eyes. Then she looks at him again and speaks:

"What must have happened is . . . I must still have been ill in my mind . . . I'd be sure I'd done something or other, whereas in fact . . . You don't realize, when you're like that . . . You think you've said things, or that things have happened, and they haven't happened at all . . . And you can't imagine how upsetting it can be when you find out . . ."

She picks up the book and looks at it.

He asks, *"Winter Afternoons*—would that have been the title of the poem?"

"Yes. Of the book, too."

They look at one another. She says, "You're right. It isn't in with the others. Nor anything like it."

She gets up and walks around the room. She doesn't touch anything. She puts the book down again. She says:

"It's only now, today, that I'm sure I didn't write it. And it's today I met you. I must forget you both, you and the poem." She smiles. "I thought I'd died that day, when I was twenty-four, but I was wrong.

Suddenly I desire your lips as if you were my first lover."

He has put his hands over his face as if to defend himself.

She asks him, "How old are you?"

"The same age as you." He looks at her unwaveringly, and she is at ease under his gaze. "I'd like you to have a copy of your book."

"No. The only real poem is inevitably the one that's lost. For me the book doesn't exist."

She looks around, looks through the open windows at the grounds, the lawns. Says, "I'd have liked to tell you something, so that it might be said . . . But I can't . . ."

"Something you've never said before?"

"Yes. But there's no need. You know it as well as I do."

"Yes. There's no need."

She smiles at him. Forgets.

"You were friendly with my father, weren't you?"

"Yes." He hesitates. "He told me what happened. He knew everything."

She smiles at the young caretaker.

"No. He didn't know everything."

"Do I?"

She thinks.

"I don't know. I don't think it's possible to know everything—even I don't know everything. I don't know what the Captain knows. You see, I lie when I talk about certain things, the things that are never talked about . . . it's almost unavoidable . . ."

She goes over to him, puts her lips on his closed eyes. Says, "I'd have liked to stay here with you until it's dark."

She straightens up, then bends and puts her lips on his. She stays like that. They stay like that, not moving, until they've come to know one another forever. Then she takes her lips away from his. And he sits as she has left him, his face in his hands, his eyes shut.

She says, "I meant to go and have another look in the bedroom over the boathouse, but that would have been silly."

He reminds her it's his room now. He says it was all redecorated the year before he came, including the walls and the floor. And nothing like that was found.

"Do you mean that, even though you didn't know what had happened, if you'd found it, either before or after my father died, it would be in the book? Even though it was unfinished?"

"I think so, yes. Even though it was unfinished."
He hesitates. "But I'm not sure. I'm not sure about
anything . . . But I think I would have sent it to the
publisher in London."

The Captain calls her from downstairs. He's going for
a drive around the north of the island—is she coming
with him? She says no, she'll stay here in the house
and grounds.

She goes out of the house through a back door.
The young caretaker is at the window. There she is.
She's crossing the lawn. In the middle she turns and
looks up at the second floor. The young caretaker is
at the window. She smiles at him. Then walks on.
She's probably making for the eucalyptus trees. But
he doesn't try to find out. Doesn't think of joining
her. He wants to remain alone in order to try to
understand, to think of her, to love her.

They left the island the next morning, and the young
caretaker didn't see her again, the woman he always
called by the name he found himself saying one night
that summer. Emily L.

Night was falling slowly, as it does after very sunny
days. Coolness rose from the river. It had the smell

of fish and spawn that you often get on an estuary.

More people arrived and went straight into the hotel restaurant.

You said, "She must feel the power within her like a kind of lost intelligence that's no use to her any more."

"And like some terrible flaw she acquired from outside her own life, she doesn't know when or how, or from whom or what?"

"Some flaw deep inside her that she's kept silent about all her life, so as to stay where she wanted to be—in the barren regions of her love for the Captain."

They didn't come back to the Isle of Wight for three years after that—that scene in the winter sitting room, with her lips on those of the young caretaker for as long as a love. The young caretaker waited for her for three years, the woman he called by his own name for her, to thwart the curiosity of those who might have known who she really was.

The startling news of the young caretaker's passion for Emily L. spread all over the island, first among the people who lived near the house, then to Newport and the gentry there, one of whom was Emily L.'s family lawyer. It was he who'd engaged the young caretaker when the man appointed by the family died. They used to meet two or three times every few months in connection with the young man's work and wages. But also to talk about Emily L.

The lawyer in Newport was the only person the young caretaker could talk to about his meeting with her in the winter sitting room. After they started talking about her the lawyer called her Emily L. too, and whenever he got a postcard from the Captain and his wife he gave them to the young caretaker to read.

Another thing they could talk about only to one another was the growing reputation of Emily L.'s poems. Neither of them could really understand their fame. It both delighted and appalled them. They were happy because every year the poems were read in more and more countries, but appalled because Emily L. herself knew nothing about it. They wondered when she would find out. They were both sure the Captain chose to sail around the Malaysian seas because the reputation of the poems probably hadn't spread that far yet.

They talked not so much about the poems as about the mystery of their ever-widening influence, due, according to the lawyer, to people more competent to judge than they were. Also about the other mystery:

how, after the disappearance of just one poem, the one about the winter light in the grounds of the house on the Isle of Wight, Emily L. couldn't write any more.

They talked about the disappearance of the poem, too. The young caretaker thought Emily L. must have known how the winter-light poem disappeared. And he was sure she'd been there, in the room, writing, when the poem came into being. Just as she'd been there, or wherever it was, day or night, at whatever time of the year, when the other poems did. The young caretaker couldn't speak in any other way about the poems Emily L. had written when both of them were young. Like her he could still see her hand holding the black pen, and he said that even if it had happened in her sleep and she'd seen it afterwards as something separate from herself, it was she herself who'd written it. The lawyer was of another opinion, or rather he expressed himself differently: the young man's way of talking made him smile. The lawyer said every poem had to have an author. You couldn't be more or less the author of a poem. You were always it completely. But the young caretaker stuck to his guns. One day, when the lawyer said he ought to see things more simply, he didn't mince his words.

He shouted out that simplicity was a crime in the case of Emily L., who was mad. And that the criminal who had murdered her was the Captain. The lawyer hadn't held the young man's anger against him.

They sat for a long time without speaking, in the gloom of the lawyer's office. Then the lawyer asked him how he knew. But the young man apologized; he'd never known anything for sure. He'd reached that conclusion of his own accord: that the Captain had murdered the poem about the winter light by throwing it on the fire. He said there were only two explanations for the poem's disappearance: either the Captain was responsible, or Emily L. was mad and only thought she'd written it. If the poem had actually existed and been put down on paper, the Captain's crime was the only solution.

The lawyer asked the young caretaker if he thought she'd thought of that. He said she must have done so, but that before long she'd realized she mustn't judge the Captain for what he'd done, because it expressed the limitations of his earthbound intelligence even more clearly than it signaled her own death.

What saddened Emily L.'s two friends most was that she'd never written anything again after what happened. But the lawyer wasn't sure. He thought she went on writing poems, but concealed the incriminating objects. The young caretaker thought it was all over, that she would never write again. Sometimes he wept unashamedly in front of the lawyer. He was almost certain that he, who knew nothing about poetry, was the only person who'd ever talked to Emily L. about what she had written. The thought was torture. Unbearable. So was the thought of the book, which—he knew it already—contained all she would ever write.

After three years, by the end of the third summer, the young caretaker was sure she'd forgotten him. And he thought his idea of the life she led in the Sunda Islands must be right.

Just before he went away there was a rumor on the Isle of Wight that she had died out there.

For the young caretaker it was a kind of hope.

But the rumor was denied.

The young caretaker left the Isle of Wight at the end of the third summer, as he'd made up his mind to do. He was still desperately in love with Emily L.

After he'd gone, the Captain and his wife came back regularly every year, up to the summer when we were all in Quillebeuf.

. . .

Night is still falling—slowly, layer by layer, behind the rows of streetlights along the road to Le Havre on the other bank. And over the river, which is turning black.

People have stopped arriving for the moment. The local people are already here, and the foreign tourists still to come will be late as usual because of the time difference. The dining room is full. Certain customers are for some reason directed to other restaurants in the area. This disagreeable task is left to the manageress's daughter. The manageress herself is in the kitchen; you can hear her voice passing on the orders.

We were still with the English couple. We hadn't spoken to them except to ask her name. We hadn't even tried. It was impossible to pierce the silence that separated them from other people.

They were still there, alone at the bar. The manageress probably kept newcomers away so that they'd be left in peace until the crew from the boat arrived. He had ordered and drunk another black Pilsen. *"The last one,"* he said. She hadn't had any more bourbon.

Now it's my turn to talk about her. I say she has an obvious gift for life. And a greater mental capacity, which makes her more alert than the Captain and quicker to understand, laugh, forget. All these small differences between her and the Captain must in the end add up to the big difference in their whole presence.

The man with fair hair and laughing eyes. He looks at the woman at the bar. In his eyes there's his eternal smile. I look at him. Tell him she'll remember him as a man with fair hair and laughing eyes, as she would a lover in Newport. Perhaps she'll say to the Captain, without any regret—regret is a thing of the past—but with the lilt of the last exile: "Like a lover I might have had when I was young, in Newport."

You say, "She won't say anything about you."

"When she looks at people she looks at them so keenly . . . Perhaps . . . who knows . . . perhaps she's understood everything for a hundred years."

"Perhaps."

You go on talking about the woman who's looking down at the floor. You can't help it. You say, "It's as if you'd given her to me." You add, "She was the one who thought of it, the blind logic of sailing around the world."

You look at her. She must keep falling asleep. Waking. Falling asleep again. You say:

"She was inevitably more delicate than he was.

94

Less sensible, but perhaps more amusing, funnier to be with. And, strangely enough, less afraid of life. More pessimistic than he was. But not so fearful of death."

I tell you to look at them: they're still on the boat here too. Even here what they're concerned with is the passage of time, the crossing of the sea. As usual at this hour, they're drunk.

You say all they have to do now is solve the problem of death. They'll solve it one evening like this. They'll decide on the place. And they'll stick to the decision. Do you have any idea where it will be? You say, "The Strait of Malacca. Suddenly. One evening." So she'll travel some more? You smile: "So rumor has it."

We look outside at the light wasting away. A whole line of tankers are heading for the sea on the ebb tide.

You say, "You're like one another, you and she. You keep looking at the river, you don't laugh. It's always very moving, a resemblance between two women who are not really alike."

I say I feel a kind of desire for her. You say you too feel as if you'd like to hold her, to feel her birdlike thinness against your skin.

We don't leave. The Captain has finished his black Pilsen. He's started talking to himself. She's still trying to find Brownie, calling him softly. *Here, boy.* She weeps. Then she forgets, laughs at things that go through her mind. Then she starts calling again. Sometimes so shrilly that the other voices in the room fall silent. But she doesn't notice anything. Her gaze plunges unfathomably again towards the floor.

You ask me if Emily L. has ever seen the young caretaker on the Isle of Wight again.

I don't think so. She asked the lawyer in Newport what had become of him. The lawyer didn't know. He'd been told he had left the island.

All I know is she asked the lawyer to try to find out how to get in touch with him. She'd written him a letter nearly four years ago. But she'd never managed to trace him, and she still had the letter, the sealed envelope. She mentioned the letter to the lawyer. She'd written to the young caretaker to say she could have loved him; she wanted him to know. She didn't know how he felt towards her; how could she have known? But she knew she herself had begun to love him during the hour they were together in the winter sitting room. Did the lawyer know?

Yes, he did. He even told her the name the young caretaker had given her: Emily L. She repeated it softly to herself, and seemed to approve of it: "Emily L. . . . yes."

At first he wouldn't take the letter. He said it was difficult for him: he was friendly with the Captain, and even more so with the young caretaker. Yes, he was especially friendly with the young man: before he met him he'd never thought anyone could be so pure-hearted. He told Emily L. he knew all about the love story between the young caretaker and her. The one that had lasted an hour, in the little sitting room in the house. And the other, the one that had taken up three years of his life, spent waiting for Emily L.

The lawyer told Emily L. he was willing to try to trace him, but only on condition that the letter wouldn't reawaken the hopes he by now had abandoned.

Emily L. thought about it. Then she told the lawyer to read the letter after she'd left his office, to read it and then do as he saw fit. To decide for himself whether it was suitable or not for the young caretaker to read. Instead of being angry, she asked this of him as if it were a great service, for which she was very grateful. She hesitated a moment, then told him she'd lost confidence in herself. She said she made mistakes sometimes while she was writing, got carried away into dangerous regions into which she ought never to have gone. So she was relying on him to decide whether this had happened in the letter.

The lawyer was extremely moved; his eyes filled with tears. But neither he nor Emily L. said anything about it.

The lawyer agreed to try to find the young caretaker and give him the letter. What was he to do with it if he couldn't find him? Emily L. told him to burn it; that was the best way of making sure it vanished forever.

As he had promised, the lawyer read the letter Emily L. had written to the young caretaker. He decided it couldn't do any harm. This is what it said:

I've forgotten the words with which to tell you. I knew them once, but I've forgotten them, and now I'm talking to you without them. Unlikely as it may seem, I'm not the sort of woman who gives herself up body and soul to the love of one person, even the person who's dearest to her in the whole world. I am someone who's unfaithful. I wish I could find the words I laid aside, to tell you that. And now some of them are coming back to me. I wanted to tell you what I think, which is that one always ought to keep oneself a place, yes, that's the word, a

private place, where one can be alone and love.
To love one knows not what, nor whom, nor
how, nor for how long. To love . . . now all
the words are suddenly coming back . . . To
set aside a place inside oneself to wait, you
never know, to wait for a love, perhaps for a
love without a person attached to it yet, but for
that and only that. For love. I wanted to tell
you you were what I had waited for. You
alone became the outer surface of my life, the
side I never see, and you will be that, the
unknown part of me, until I die. Don't ever
answer this. And please don't hope to see me.
                                        Emily L.

The lawyer found an address in South America. He
mailed the letter. But it was returned. He sent it to
all the British embassies in the whole American continent. It always came back. But he didn't burn it.

We look again at the slowly dying day.

    You say, "What's in that letter can't be understood
by the reader. It must have been read just once by
a writer who thought he understood it and put it into
a book. And then forgot it."

    "Yes, I think there are things like that. For instance, in letters that are part of an author's work, and yet are different from what he knows and intends. Indistinguishable from the other things in the book, and yet alien to it."

I tell you, "My love for you was fearsome."

There's mistrust in your eyes again. You shift your gaze to beyond the cliffs. You say, "To say that is as untrue as to say I don't love you."

I look at you. Try to see you. Can't look at you.

"Sometimes I still think perhaps I don't love you. And nothing occurs to me to prove I'm wrong. I really do believe I might not have loved you. Then it all comes back. You make the same mistake in reverse. The thought must sometimes strike you that perhaps you do love me. Or rather that in what you feel for me there might sometimes be traces of love, impossible as that may seem. But I'm probably wasting my breath. When that happens to you, if it ever does, you probably won't know anything about it."

"I'll know somehow or other."

"You'll understand the story like Henry James's heroes—when it's over. You'll find out externally that feeling exists. It'll take a long time to reach your consciousness. Everything around you will have changed, and you'll still be wondering why. You won't recognize anything. You won't know anything.

Until the time comes when you too transform the situation into a book or a personal relationship."

"So you don't think I could have understood Emily L.'s letter?"

"That I might contemplate a love other than my love for you?—you wouldn't have been able to bear to understand it."

"And you—you wanted to have one absolute and perfect love, and at the same time to have another, to help out."

"Not quite . . . I didn't either hope for it or want to supplement it. I just wanted to write about it."

"I can understand that."

"All writers can."

I look at you. You ask me what's the matter. You're always rather alarmed when I look at you. I say nothing's the matter, I was just enjoying looking at you.

"I don't know if love's a feeling. Sometimes I think it's a matter of seeing. Seeing you."

There's a hiatus in the noise, in the light, in the arrival and departure of cars. The rhythm of the ferry is different. There are fewer crossings in the evening. Almost everyone is in the restaurant. The manageress of the bar has come to collect the money for the

English couple's drinks, and for ours. She tells us to take our time, she'll only be in the kitchen lending a hand.

After she goes there's a long silence. And then the woman at the bar starts talking about Brownie again. She says it's such a shame he's dead. The Captain shouts, begs her to stop: *"Please—forget about Brownie!"* She says it was the manageress of the Marine who mentioned him first—and starts talking about him again. Brownie was a marvelous dog, *"the nicest one we ever had,"* in her opinion. He'd said so himself—the nicest one in England. *"My God!"* roars the Captain. But she goes on. It was such a shame he always tried to run away whenever they were in port. You had to admit it, *"he was no good at guarding the boat, poor Brownie."* The Captain bursts out laughing. He says Brownie was much too small to guard anything. They both laugh heartily. Then she tells the Captain he ought to let her talk about Brownie sometimes; it will help her get over it.

She shuts her eyes. She's stopping herself from crying.

I look at her motionless body. Her legs could still be beautiful. Not her feet, though—they're shrunken, atrophied. She's let her shoes drop off—

little flat children's sandals made of pink canvas. Her clothes are the sort young people wear, made of artificial satin or Japanese silk. They're rather dirty. Her hair is the color of dust: it's been hennaed at ports of call and the roots are grey.

On the fingers of her left hand she wears all the rings, gold and diamonds, that came to her from her people in Devon. That's the hand she uses to pick up the bourbon. A sip.

With her eyes closed she moves closer to him. Without a word. He holds himself very straight until their bodies touch. She stays there, leaning against him. He drinks his black Pilsen, not looking at us now. She takes the sip of bourbon. Puts the glass down again. He drinks the dark beer again, empties the tankard. But this time she hasn't touched the bourbon. To bridge the gap between them now they resort to drink. He, being rather conventional, is perhaps slightly embarrassed, but only slightly, by her going on about the boat, and the faint impropriety of her leaning her body on his, at their age, in front of people.

You said, "She's at the end of her life."

When we came back the next day, they were gone. We didn't ask after them from the people at the bar.

Back in the car you said, "The Koreans—it would make a good title for a book."

I told you I loved you. You never answered such insane talk.

Afterwards I talked about them again. Afterwards, after we'd left Quillebeuf, but I can't remember when. But I do know it was on the journey back. I talked about seeing them again. I said it was possible we might see them again, that they might come back to Quillebeuf one last time and we might come across them, either in the Café de la Marine or in the square. So we'd have to go back to Quillebeuf, if only to find they weren't there. I said I thought we'd even have to go specially to see them if we found out they'd taken to calling in at Quillebeuf, as they did at Venice, and sometimes still, perhaps, at the Isle of Wight. Always supposing she hadn't died that night.

I said, "All the same, you can't help wondering what on earth those Koreans were doing in Quillebeuf. Seeing that Quillebeuf is scarcely mentioned in the tourist guides, and that it's hard to get to unless you know the roads, and that there are no big hotels or casinos and no swimming pool, you can't help wondering what the Koreans were doing there unless they were up to no good." But you weren't listening. And I stopped talking about them. That was the end of the Koreans. They ceased to exist for either of us.

We talked about people in general. We said all the people one saw in bars and boats and trains were unforgettable, even if one forgot them afterwards. Not people in newspaper photographs or films, but those alone on buses or in bars in the evening—all, whether they were workers or not, exhausted by the day that had just gone by, all plunged in the somber exaltation of the life within.

By then you no longer loved me. You probably never had. You were thinking of leaving me; it was a question of money for you, of earning some money—you never said "earning your living." And I was already embarked on the project I'd told you about that day, of writing that story, but was held back from being entirely caught up in it because of the love I still had for you; but anyhow, I was already turned in the direction of doing it one day. And you knew all about that project and that feeling, but you never once talked to me about them.

. . .

As usual when we were coming back from Quillebeuf, we talked about the light on the plateau. We couldn't make out why it was so beautiful, so special. At that hour it had lost its brilliance; it wasn't altogether separate from the dark; it was almost supernatural.

We were a long way past the plateau now. Instead of taking the expressway at Pont-Audemer, we'd turned off towards Foulbec and Berville—we wanted to go past the bay. At Berville we made for what used to be the harbor of Rouen. You come upon the bay quite suddenly. After a lot of little clumps of trees you emerge on what we call the German factory, a huge empty hulk with shattered windows. Tonight the wind isn't whistling through it. We stop.

The Seine is there by the factory. The three waterways: two canals, and in the middle the river itself.

We often stop here. The ground is strewn with broken glass from the windows. We walk over to the twisted remains of the metal landing stage where the German boats used to take on material for building their sea walls and forts: blocks of granite and red bricks. In the distance, the Sainte-Adresse light through the summer mist. You are looking towards the lights of Le Havre. You don't speak. Perhaps you're crying; I don't know. Perhaps. You say you'd like to know some more about the people from the Isle of Wight. I say I don't really know much more. You say you don't either. One last tanker sails by. Its decks are lit up as if it were the middle of the night. You say the love story took the place of the sailing around the world.

One day the young caretaker arrived at the lawyer's office in Newport. They were very glad to see one another again. The lawyer gave the young caretaker the letter that Emily L. had written him eight years ago and that had been around North and South America several times before coming back to Newport. He hadn't thrown it on the fire as she'd asked him to do if he couldn't find the young caretaker. The lawyer showed the young caretaker into the room adjoining his office where people were left to read the wills of their departed. The young man stayed in there for a long while with his letter.

They went for a walk together around Emily L.'s house. They didn't talk about the letter. It was autumn, the weather was fine, they walked for a long while along the paths the young Emily L. used to take. The lawyer told the young caretaker that the Captain and his wife no longer came to the Isle of Wight every year. The young caretaker liked the thought that she'd abandoned the Isle of Wight at almost the same time he had. They went into the house to look at the little winter sitting room again. Many of the things in it had been either stolen or taken by visitors, and the young caretaker and the lawyer liked that too, the sacking of Emily L.'s private life.

The young caretaker talked about his own life. Eight years back, the same year she'd written him the letter, he'd gone to the little Malaysian seas to try to find Emily L., to steal her and take her away and not give her back, perhaps to kill her. He'd hired a yacht and two Javanese seamen and called at all the ports in Borneo, Java, and Malacca. He said he was looking for an Englishwoman who lived all the year round in this part of the tropics with her husband, on a yacht flying the British flag. For three months he sailed around the little seas of the South Pacific and among the islands, then along the coast of Indochina and past the whole Malay Peninsula down to Sumatra. That's where they'd searched most thoroughly, in the Java Sea, among the curves of the Indonesian Cyclades, and then towards Pontianak and in the Natuna archipelago, on the edge of the China Sea. It was a place where people led the same irregular existence day and night. Many were awake at night on the boats in these archipelagos, on yachts and junks and liners too. It was close to the equator, and on the liners they always celebrated crossing it. The young caretaker went to many such parties in the still night of the tropics. The mist shut in the sounds and the music and turned the sea into a place of conspiracy, an atmosphere that must have been hard to shake off once you'd lived in it. It was on an Australian freighter moored at a port of call on its way to Korea that the young caretaker saw Emily L., among about twenty couples dancing on a dais on the upper deck. She was dancing with one of the ship's officers and wearing her old white and blue dress. The young caretaker didn't look to see if the Captain was there. He just looked at her. He recognized the long sunburned legs, the dawning smile arrested in a profound sweetness, her way of half-closing her eyes and remaining safe in her solitude. The young caretaker stayed there motionless watching the dance floor until the first glimmers of dawn. Then the orchestra stopped playing and he escaped. He went back to his hired yacht and hid there under the straw awning for several days. Waiting, as he thought, until he could go up to her on the quayside. But when he made up his mind to go out again he couldn't see the liner any more, nor any of the other small boats around it. The harbor was empty. Then the young caretaker lay down on the deck of his hired boat and asked for his body to be taken to Singapore. For several days he lay there dead on the deck. His money and papers were stolen. The Singapore police found him on the deserted ship, and had him repatriated to a town in Latin America that he'd mentioned in his sleep. There he found himself still alive, and there he stayed, got married, set up a business, and had children. After his awakening, Emily L. was dead for him for over a year. He had lost their story. Lost her eyes, her voice, her closed eyes against his mouth, then her lips against his, and her hands; but especially her closed eyes. Emily L.'s eyes remained open and sightless for months. And then one night he awoke again and the story was there once more. It began again between them, without any possibility of evolution, as fragile now as Emily L.'s letter, and, like it, stronger than death.

It was strange—we could no longer tell if it was night or not. Over the river the sky was lighter again, as if the dusk had recovered its power.

Everyone had said it was going to be a glorious summer.

All the waters were calm, those of the sea and those of the river alike. The fresh water was usually slowed down in its descent to the sea by what I called the great smooth cables of the swell, which barred its way from one bank to the other. But not that evening. As far as the eye could see the river was flowing unhindered into the sea. It was as if the waters were borne along by sleep. No doubt about it, we hadn't been wrong, it was still day. The light in the sky didn't belong to the night, it was still coming from the sun. Tonight was going to be a typical night of early summer. Still cool towards the dawn. It was June.

I don't remember if we had dinner.

I don't remember what we did between the time we left the canal by the German factory until the time we went to bed.

I do remember there was a kind of tranquillity stretching all over the sea and over us.

That night you didn't go out roaming the big hotels and the hills. You stayed in. I went to bed.

Your body and mine were enclosed in the same space. You always fell asleep before I did, you slept well. That always reassured me, because night brought you oblivion of the life you led with me and that you wanted to give up.

And then I woke. I called you, you didn't answer. So I got up. I went to your door and called out; perhaps

111

you were asleep, I don't know, it didn't occur to me. In the end you said, "What's the matter?" I said I wanted to tell you it wasn't enough to write well or badly, to create writings that are beautiful or even very beautiful, it wasn't enough any longer to produce a book that people read to satisfy a personal and not a communal appetite. And it wasn't enough to write like that, either—to make people believe it was done without thought, merely by following your hand; just as it was too much to write simply with the mind in charge, supervising the activity of madness. It's not enough—philosophy and morals and ordinary examples of the human race (what about dogs, for example?) are not enough, they don't get through to the body that's reading the story and wants to know the story right from the start, and that with every reading is ignorant of more than it was ignorant of already.

And I said one ought to write without making corrections, not necessarily at full tilt, no, but at one's own pace and in accordance with what one is experiencing at the time; one ought to eject what one writes, manhandle it almost, yes, treat it roughly, not try to trim profusion but let it be part of the whole, and not tone down anything either, whether its speed or its slowness, just leave everything as it is when it appears.

One of the most important literary figures in France, Marguerite Duras is best known in the United States for her novel *The Lover* and her memoir *The War,* and for her brilliant filmscript *Hiroshima, Mon Amour.* She is also the author of many other acclaimed novels and screenplays. Born in Indochina in 1914, she now lives in Paris.